The Kona-Town Musicians

Library of Congress Catalog Card Number. 97-076180

ISBN 0-9633493-6-8

First Printing, 1998

Graphic Layout by J. Jay West,
Aries Graphics, Kamuela, Hawaii

Printing Coordinator, Dick Lyday,
Heritage Graphics, Inc., Honolulu

Available from:
Pacific Greetings
65-1285 Puu Opelu Road
Kamuela, HI 96743
(808) 885-4439   e-mail = hlhall@ilhawaii.net

Printed in Hong Kong

The Kona-Town Musicians

The happy Hawaiian version of
the Brothers Grimm fairy tale,
The Bremen-Town Musicians

Story adaptation
and
illustrations
by
Pat Hall

~~~Pacific Greetings~~~

Kamuela, Hawaii

Many years ago, donkeys were used instead of tractors at harvest time to carry big sacks of coffee beans on the coffee farms of Hawaii. On one of these farms there lived an old donkey.

He had worked hard all his life on the steep mountainsides of Mauna Loa, but he was now too old to carry the heavy sacks, so his master was going to get rid of him.

"I think I'd better get out of here while I still have a chance," said the old donkey.

"I have a beautiful bray and I'm sure if I go down to Kona-town I can join some musicians and sing for the tourists."

He had walked part way down the mountain when he met an old, beat-up pig-hunting dog beside the road.

"You sure look lost and sad. What's wrong?" said the old donkey.

"I'm too old to keep up with the younger dogs on the wild boar hunts, so my master just leaves me behind," whined the old dog.

"I'm sure you still have a great bark. Why not join me? I'm going down to Kona-town to sing for the tourists," said the old donkey.

The old dog thought that was a great idea. It sure beat the hard work of hunting wild pigs in the rain forest. So he trotted off with the donkey.

The two old animals traveled on a bit further down the mountain when they came upon a scruffy old tom cat.

"My you look unhappy, what's wrong?" asked the old donkey.

"I'm too old now to catch the fast little mice, so my mistress won't care for me any more," grumbled the old cat.

"I'm sure you still have a nice healthy yowl," said the old donkey. "Why not join us? We are going down to Kona-town to sing for the tourists."

This sounded like a much better way to make a living than chasing mice. So the cat got up and eagerly followed the two musicians.

Soon the donkey, dog and cat came
upon a frazzled old fighting rooster.
"What's wrong old rooster?" asked the donkey.

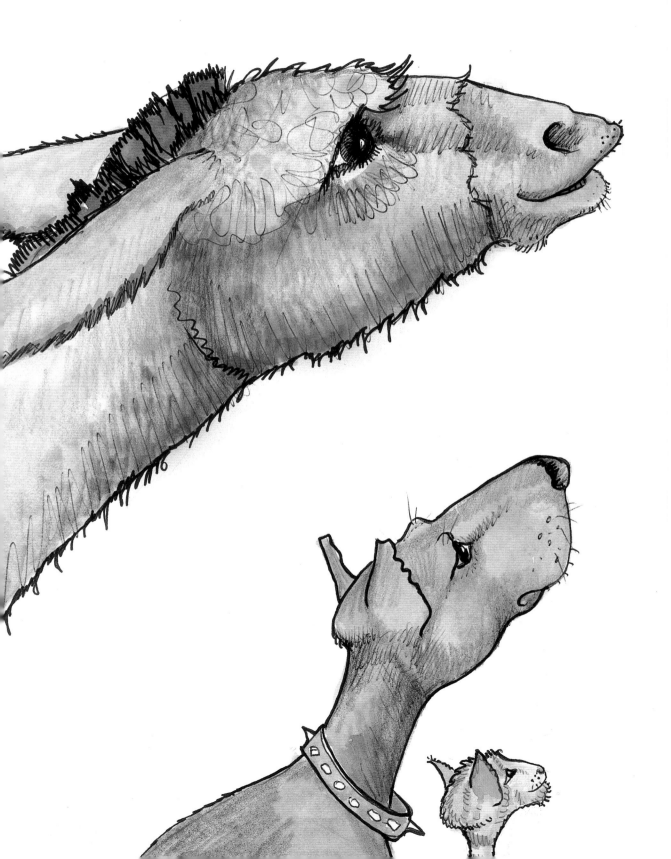

"I almost lost my last chicken fight and I'm sure my master is eventually going to make me into chicken luau," said the old rooster.

"Come with us, we are going down to Kona-town to sing for the tourists. I'm sure your crow is still just as loud as ever, and singing for the tourists is a whole lot better than flavoring a pot of chicken luau!" said the old donkey.

The rooster really liked the donkey's idea.
So he flew up on the donkey's back and went
along with them.

It was getting late when they reached the beach just outside of Kona-town. The sun had gone down and they were tired and hungry. They smelled food and saw a friendly campfire down the beach. The four old animals crept up silently and saw several young boys eating lomi lomi salmon, Spam musubi, rice and stew, while telling each other scary Hawaiian ghost stories.

"Let's try out our singing on these nice young boys!" whispered the donkey.

So they positioned themselves to achieve the maximum theatrical effect. The dog stood on the donkey's back, the cat got up on the dogs back, and the rooster flew up onto the very top. Then, on cue, they all started to sing at once. The donkey let out a long strong bray, the dog howled, the cat yowled and the rooster crowed and furiously flapped his wings to add a little extra drama.

When all of this happened the boys leaped to their feet and yelled "Ghosts!!" and ran off in a cloud of sand leaving all their food and their warm fire behind. The four old animals were surprised at the boys reaction, but thought it was nice of them to leave all that wonderful food just sitting there on the beach.

"What a wonderful life this is going to be," said the old tom cat after he finished off the lomi lomi salmon and curled up by the fire.

"What a wonderful way to make a living," said the old pig dog as he wolfed down the last of the stew and Spam musubi.

"What a beautiful place to live," said the old donkey sharing a large pan of rice with the rooster.

These four musicians still work the beaches near Kona-town, and on a quiet warm Kona evening you can hear the donkey bray, the rooster crow, the dog bark, and the cat yowl.